There's always a choice in life; either you take it or you leave it!

Tenike Marie

Planet Phenexus

A CIP catalogue record for this title is available from the British Library.

ISBN 9781786298621 (Paperback)
ISBN 9781786298638 (Hardback)
ISBN 9781786298648 (eBook)

www.austinmacauley.com

First Published (2017)
Austin Macauley Publishers Ltd.
25 Canada Square
Canary Wharf
London
E14 5LQ

Let me tell you an adventurous story about Tami Hall, who was twenty-one and lived in a small house with her mother, Mirian, and her six brothers and sisters, Fiona, Morgan, Michael, Harvey, Talisha, and Tanarla, whose ages ranged from ten to twenty-three. They were like any ordinary family, the only difference being that they always felt the need to help others, even if they couldn't quite help themselves.

Tami's siblings lived normal lives, but deep down, each felt different, as if he or she did not belong on Earth. Tami always felt connected with the sun, as she was always distracted by it. After having indescribable emotions about the unique connection she felt, Tami would talk about the sun for days to her friends and family. Her mother advised her not to talk about the sun too much, as people would start to think she was crazy. After this advice, Tami decided to keep it bottled up and spoke about it with no one. Mirian knew exactly how Tami was feeling, for she felt the same way about the moon. Mirian believed she could almost communicate with the moon and draw energy from it.

When Mirian was eight years old, she was playing in the garden, having the best time of her life.

The garden was flourishing, the sun was shining, and everyone was content. Mirian wanted to add to the amusement. She ran with excitement towards a ball that was inside the house. As she was running, a harsh light materialised in the corners of her eyes. The light made her eyes watery and crystal-like. She stopped running and rubbed her eyes profusely. Looking towards the bright light, she managed to get a brief look and saw that the shape of the phenomenon was spherical. Mirian looked to see if there were any witnesses to the phenomenon. Unfortunately, there were not.

She forced herself to believe it was her imagination. As she strolled to the ball, her perplexed state of mind took over her body. She had no control over her thoughts or her bodily functions; a light beam materialised, hurling the ball into her mother's favourite vase.

Her mother came rushing into the house in disbelief at the pieces scattered over a wide distance. The bewildering mind state vanished. Mirian was crying because she had jumped back into reality not knowing what was going on. She saw her mother shouting at her, but she could not fathom why her mother's favourite vase was broken.

Mirian's mother sent her to her room; it was hard for Mirian to stop crying as her rage soared. She slammed her bedroom door with more force than physics would be able to explain. With her anger increasing with no limit she threw herself onto her bed, crying. As she covered her eyes, she suddenly saw unique colours slowly appearing through the cracks of her hands, catching her attention.

Mirian mumbled to herself, "This was the same thing I saw before the vase broke but this time the colours are very different. This thing is more than likely the reason I got in trouble." She put her hand through the lights without feeling anything. She tried her hardest to ignore the light, thinking it would vanish like the bright yellow light she saw before the vase broke. The light was stagnant, so Mirian closed her eyes and clenched her fists.

Visualising the light getting smaller, Mirian immediately got a headache because of the time she spent containing such a large power that came with heavy presence. The mental encapsulation attempt failed, causing Mirian's legs to capitulate to the pressure of the explosion. The explosion spread over a wide distance, resulting in a city power cut. Mirian knew at that point that she was special in some way.

As the years went on, Mirian lived her life, forgetting about the past completely after having seven wonderful kids by her first and true love. After fourteen years, her husband, Aaron, died in a traffic accident on his way to work. Not long after that, things got hard for Mirian because she had to look after her kids by herself. But no matter how hard things got, Mirian always found a way to support and care for her children, who were her pride and joy. As the years passed, things started to become shaky for all of Mirian's kids. Without a warning or sign, weird things started to happen to each of them.

Mirian organised a birthday party for the youngest of her sons, Michael. He had so much fun on his special day with all his friends; he received a lot of toys and gadgets. By eight that night, it was time for his friends to go home because everyone had school in the morning, so he said his goodbyes. He went upstairs to his room with all his new and cool presents. Mirian shouted from downstairs, asking Michael to get into the bath so he could get up early for school tomorrow. As Tami was walking out of her room from downstairs she heard her mother ask her to call up to Michael and tell him to get out of the bath. As Tami started to walk up the stairs to tell Michael to get out, her phone began to ring and she saw it was her best friend calling. She quickly ran back into her room completely forgetting about her brother and what her mother had asked her to do. Mirian called out to Tami asking her if Michael came out the bath, but because Tami was distracted by the conversation she was having with her best friend, she lied to Mirian telling her that Michael came out the bath and that he was in bed. Mirian thanked Tami for her help and went upstairs into her bedroom and went to bed.

The next morning, Mirian went upstairs into the bathroom to brush her teeth when she saw Michael in the bath underwater. His skin was a pale blue. She started to panic when she saw that he was unresponsive as she was trying to wake him up. So she quickly called for an ambulance and when they arrived, Mirian rushed straight to the bathroom. When the paramedics followed Mirian, Michael's body was no longer there. Everyone was looking around for his body with great confusion.

While they were still searching around one of the paramedics heard light movement coming from the next room. One of the paramedics left the bathroom to check it out. That's when they saw Michael sitting on his bed, getting himself ready for school as he was running late. Mirian couldn't explain what happened that morning or how he survived. That day was never spoken of, as they wanted to just put their feelings and experiences behind them and try to live a normal life. But as the years went on, it got harder and harder for the family. They all had something mysterious happen to them. It was hard to ignore the signs about their unique gifts.

Talisha Hall was the third youngest of her siblings, a free-spirited seventeen-year-old. She was always with her best friend, Alex Brown. They were almost inseparable and very much into magic, arts, and crafts. But her life was no longer normal on 27 August, a Friday afternoon. Talisha and Alex were in class when their teacher, Mrs Breetox, announced that the school would be holding a talent show. Alex and Talisha were the first ones to put their names on the list. They began to practice hard because they wanted to stand out from everyone else. Two days later, it was the day of the talent show. Talisha and Alex could not wait to show off their performance, so they prepared themselves to be best performers.

After the last performance finished, Alex and Talisha walked onstage and began their magic trick. Talisha prepared herself to get into a box with a padlock on it. Alex closed the lid and locked it. When he completed the first part of the trick, Alex looked around. The theatre was full of people. He started to sweat and breathe hard. Suddenly, the whole place became quiet. Alex passed out on stage due to having a panic attack. "Quick," Mrs Breetox said frantically, "call for help." When the paramedics arrived, they saw Alex's helpless body on the floor and carried him to the ambulance. But because of what happened to Alex, all the attention was on him. Everyone forgot about Talisha, who was still locked up in the box. And because Talisha's mum was unable to make it to her daughter's talent show, she was left in the dark too, not knowing what happened to Talisha. She glanced down at her watch and realised that Talisha should've been home an hour ago. Mirian became anxious and quickly called the school to find out when the talent show finished and where Talisha could be.

Principal Eden asked, "How can I help you?"

Almost out of breath, she asked the principal, "Has the talent show finished? Do you know if Talisha is still at the school? It's five thirty, and she's not home yet. I'm extremely worried."

Mr Eden replied with a positive attitude regarding finding out where Talisha might be. Before they got off the phone, Mr Eden promised he would ring every lecturer and student to see if anyone knew where she had been. When they said their goodbyes and got off the phone, Mr Eden got up from his office chair and made his way down the long corridor and into the main hall where the talent show had taken place. He saw Mrs

Breetox, one of Talisha's teachers. He went to her and asked if she had seen Talisha. Mrs Breetox froze and then pointed to where she last saw Talisha, explaining to Mr Eden that Talisha must still be locked up in the box that Alex had put her in.

Principle Eden ran towards the box with a great force and started to unlock the keypad. His heart started to beat heavily, his imagination taking him on a ride of terror. When he slowly took off the box lid, he saw Talisha and was absolutely shocked. He had thought she would be dead, but she had two hands behind her head and looked Principal Eden straight in the eyes, and said with a calming voice, "What took you so long?" Doing some fast calculation, he realised that she must've been in the box for about an hour. Principle Eden thought to himself that it would have been impossible for someone to stay in a box that was sealed and to still be conscious.

Mr Eden and Mrs Beetox were shocked and amazed. Mr Eden escorted Talisha home. And on his drive back to the school, he thought to himself that Talisha was special.

Two days after Talisha's mysterious event, something strange happened to Talisha's little sister, something so strange that she couldn't tell anyone about the night of her birthday. Tanarla Hall was a very quiet and humble girl who always kept herself to herself whenever she went to school or out with friends. But something out of the ordinary and unexplainable happened to Tanarla on her fourteenth birthday. On 29 August, Mirian organised a day at the cinema with her friends so she could celebrate her birthday with her friends she loved most.

As Tanarla and her friends were getting ready at her house, Mirian was getting the car ready so she could drop Tanarla and her three close friends off at the cinema. Once they finished getting dressed, Tanarla and her friends ran straight to Mirian's car, where she was waiting for them. Because they had taken so long to get ready, they only had half an hour to get to the cinema. Mirian had to rush to the cinema because she did not want them to be late for their movie. They made it just in time. Tanarla rushed out the car and quickly thanked Mirian for the lift. When the movie finished, Tanarla and her three friends said their goodbyes and went their separate ways. Tanarla looked around the cinema car park but was unable to see her mother. So she sat outside the cinema and waited an hour for her mother. Getting impatient, she looked in her bag for her phone, but she remembered that she had left it in her mother's car. It started to get dark and cold.

Tanarla got up from where she was sitting and began to walk home. When she was three blocks away from her home, she began to run because it started to rain heavily. As Tanarla was about to cross the road she began to look left and right, and realised no cars were heading in her direction. Suddenly a car appeared from nowhere driving at full speed, which almost hit Tanarla. As she saw the car coming, she started to scream while she was in a defending position as her eyes were closed. She realised that she did not hear the car anymore. She opened her eyes and noticed that she was standing outside her home. Tanarla thought she was dreaming; she believed it was impossible to be in two places at once. As the image of the car was running through her mind, she thought of her home and her loved ones, realizing that she was outside the place she loved most. She didn't know what happened that night or why, but she strongly believed that she had teleported.

The next morning after the weird event took place near her home, Tanarla woke up in what she thought was her bed and realised that she was in someone else's house. She was alerted by the screaming and shouting that startled her, and she turned around and saw two young girls of five and twelve staring at her. The two little girls' parents ran as fast as lightning when they heard their daughters' distressing screams coming from their guest room. Their hearts were beating extremely fast when they started to imagine the worst. Getting closer to the room, the father grabbed the nearest object that he saw, which was an old fireplace poker resting on the side of the wall of the staircase. When they reached the room, they saw their two girls looking directly at Tanarla, who was scared and crying her heart out. The two parents shifted their bodies to where she was lying and asked her what her name was and where she was from. Tanarla slowly looked up to where they were standing, their two kids between them. She sat up from the bed and said with a shaky voice that she didn't mean to startle the kids as she began to wipe her tears away.

The mother of the two girls sat next to Tanarla and gave her a hug, saying in a calm voice that she believed every word she said. The mother asked Tanarla if she wanted to freshen up and have breakfast with them. But as much as that sounded good to her, she was still wondering how she got there. She pulled the mother's hands towards her and asked her where she was. The father explained in a concerned voice that she was in Santa Barbara. Tanarla was in a state of shock when she heard where she was. She ran towards the nearest window and saw thick white snow, which she hadn't seen for a little while. The mother placed her hands on her shoulders and asked her if she was from England, due to the strong English accent. She turned to her and said, "Yes, I was born and raised in England, with my mother and older and younger siblings."

As he was walking out of the room, she asked her husband to take the girls and get them breakfast. Then she turned and asked Tanarla how she managed to get into her guest bed. Tanarla closed her eyes and told her what happened to her the night before. She added that she went home and went straight to bed, and then the next morning, she explained that she woke up in the guest room. The woman held her hands and asked her if she had a unique power that she didn't know about. When she was listening to what the woman was saying, she built up enough courage and told her that she had weird things happen to her.

The woman told Tanarla to stand up and try to think of the people she loved and the home that she missed very much. Tanarla asked the woman what her name was. The woman smiled and said her name was Aerial. Tanarla smiled back and gave her a big hug. Then she closed her eyes and thought about the place that she loved the most. Aerial was still in a hugging position when she realised that Tanarla was no longer with her. She smiled to herself when she began to walk out of the room. She looked back at where she had been standing with Tanarla and closed the door behind her.

Tanarla did not end up in her mother's house. She ended up in a place that she last thought about before she disappeared from Aerial's home. She ended up appearing in the middle of the Broadway ice skating ring. Luckily, it wasn't opening time. Her body was lying flat on the ice skating ring, her hands starting to freeze, and then she had an image in her head of her bedroom. A man's whistling coming from a distance distracted her. It started to get louder, meaning that the man was getting closer to Tanarla. She heard the doors opening and thought about her bed. She disappeared as one of the cleaners entered the ice skating ring.

When Tanarla opened her eyes, she was in her bed, exactly what she had imagined. When she looked at the time, she saw that it was only seven in the morning. She left her room and saw her older sister, Fiona, walking out of the bathroom, and she rushed towards her to tell her what happened the other night and where she woke up in the early hours of the morning. But unfortunately, Fiona had little time because she was running late for work. At twenty-three, Fiona was the oldest of her siblings, and she was a person people could rely on. Because she was kind-hearted and sensible, she worked as a nurse at the Saint Elisabeth Hospital. Caring for the sick was one of her greatest passions in life, feeling like a gift to her.

One day Fiona noticed that she could control the weather. On a miserable Sunday afternoon as she left work, she realised that the rain was not easing up. Walking home, she started to pray, asking God or someone to help the weather improve. By the time Fiona finished her prayer, she noticed that the rain had stopped. Fiona wondered whether it was her doing or just a coincidence. She paused and decided to test herself. She whispered to herself, "Make it rain; let it rain." She repeated this twice and then realised that little droplets were hitting her shoulders and her face. She was overwhelmed and confused at the same time, unable to believe what she was capable of doing.

During the next few days, she tried to show her siblings and mother that she was able to control the weather. But every time she tried to show them, nothing happened, making her look crazy. One evening she was leaving work quite annoyed because she had to stay at work for an extra hour without any extra pay. As she was walking closer to the entry doors, she saw how hot and beautiful the weather looked outside. After she went to the front desk to sign out of the hospital and exited the premises, dark grey clouds started to appear in the sky and it started to rain. She didn't notice the weather change, as she was still upset with doing an extra hour of work for no compensation.

As she started to walk to the bus stop where she normally waited for the bus to take her home, she saw one of her old school friends. They spoke and exchanged phone numbers, which made Fiona forget about work, and the gloomy sky looked bright and hot again. Her long-term friend made a comment about the English weather playing up all the time, which got Fiona's attention. She was still convinced that she was able to control the weather through her emotions.

She saw her bus coming from a distance and gave her friend a big hug goodbye. After boarding the bus and taking a seat, she tested herself by listening to one of her favourite songs of all time, Angel Olsen's "Windows". Putting her headphones into her ears, she began to listen to the lyrics of the song, and suddenly tears started to roll down her face. The beautiful weather immediately became dark and gloomy, and it began to rain hard. Fiona was definitely convinced that she had a unique gift, but this time she kept it to herself.

Arriving home from work, she went into the kitchen and found her family sitting around the table. Her mother asked her what was she smiling about. She simply replied in a relaxed voice that she had a good day. When the weather changed for the third time without any warning, Fiona heard Tami mention to her mother how weird the weather was that day. Fiona walked upstairs and continued to smile to herself because she felt so special.

The days continued to pass, and all those in the Hall household were doing well. Tami, the third oldest of the siblings, was an adventurous girl who loved nature. Tami was a full-time student who studied forensic science at the University of Cambridge. She loved the fact she would be able to help solve crimes, also knowing that she could help somebody get justice, which would help bring peace to the world. One night when she finished university late, she missed the last train. She had to walk home by herself because the rest of her university friends lived nearby.

She saw three boys on bikes peddling quickly towards her and knew they were planning to take her bag. They had their hands reached out to grab it. But Tami's sharp instincts allowed her to manage to position her body away from the boys. Electricity started to charge through her body, which caused her to electrocute the three boys. She couldn't explain what happened, but she knew that the electricity came from her. She made sure that they were okay when she saw burns on their arms and face she quickly called the police and an ambulance.

When the police officers arrived, she told them what happened and how they were planning to rob her. One of the medical members unexpectedly went up to one of the officers and pulled him to the side, away from Tami. The officer looked back at one of the boys, glanced at her, and then started to look at the medical report that he was holding after receiving it from the medical nurse. Tami heard the officer thank the nurse. Returning to

Tami, he pulled her to the side and began to ask her what happened with the three boys. The medical report was stating that the three boys had third-degree burns all over their backs and arms. Tami was in shock when she was listening to what the police officer was telling her. She interrupted the officer and asked if she could go home and talk to him tomorrow, when she feels more relaxed. The officer agreed and offered to drop her home. When they arrived, he made an appointment for her to see him so she could finish off her statement and answer the questions he'd asked.

As she left the car, her mother rushed out and held her tightly as she started to search her body to see if she was hurt. But Tami wasn't in the mood for attention, and she hurried into the house, leaving her mother talking to the officer. Her sisters and brothers started to ask her questions about what took place, but she was speechless and began to head up the stairs towards her bedroom, her face blank and in shock as she passed her siblings to get to her room.

The next morning, Mirian woke up Tami so that she could drop her at the police station so she could finish giving her statement and answer the questions that the police officer had been trying to ask her the night before. As Tami got up from bed, she felt ill and weak, but she still managed to have her shower and cereal. After she finished her breakfast, she rushed to the car and saw her mother waiting on her. When she started to open the car door, the same electricity that was coming from her body appeared again, which caused her to shock herself.

She started to rub her hands where she was shocked. Her mother opened the door for her and told her to get into the car, as they only had a few minutes to get there.

During the drive, her mother asked her what happened the previous night and how the three guys at the scene got badly injured. Tami started to get flashbacks from the incident and she began to rub her head intensively, telling her mother that she didn't want to talk about it. So Mirian dropped it and left Tami alone.

They arrived at the police station just in time for her ten o'clock appointment. Mirian stayed in the waiting room while Tami followed the officer inside one of the rooms. He introduced himself as Officer Cory. In the middle of the room was an average-sized table with two black chairs on either side. Cory sat down opposite Tami and brought out a pen and a paper, beginning to ask her the questions that she had tried to avoid and block out of her mind. But she managed to tell Officer Cory what happened, although she made up a lie, saying that when they tried to rob her and failed, they tried to ride away on their bikes. When a man saw what they were planning to do, and he started to run after them. They jumped off their bikes and ran into an alleyway that was cut off by a high voltage fence. They climbed over the fence and were electrocuted.

After hearing Tami's statement about what happened to the boys, Officer Cory asked Tami to describe what the man looked like and the time he appeared at the scene. Tami made up a description of a person who wasn't real and lied about the time that she saw the man chasing after the three boys. When she finished her make-believe story, Officer Cory thanked Tami for her participation. He told her not to worry, adding that everything would be all right and that they would catch the man that Tami said she saw for a statement.

As she was walking out of the room, Tami felt much better and more relaxed. Whilst Tami and Mirian headed out of the police station, Tami promised herself that she would never lie again, especially to a police officer.

The next morning, Tami felt like herself again when she realised that she wasn't electrocuting herself. As she was walking downstairs from her bedroom, she saw her second oldest sister, Morgan, who went to the Havering College. Tami asked her if she had classes that day, which she did, and Tami walked past her to get into the kitchen. Morgan said goodbye to Tami as she closed the front door to make her way to college.

Morgan was a very outspoken person, and because she was so open, she was bullied at college for it. Mirian had to pay close attention to her, because the bullying was affecting her college work. So every day when she left her house for college, she always had to call her mother to let her know that she'd left the house and that she was safe.

One morning when Morgan was walking to college, she saw her bullies crossing the road. She tried to run to another block, but she was too slow. Her bullies got hold of her and started to pick on her, which turned physical and led her to have two black eyes, a split lip, and a swollen face. Once her bullies saw the damage that they had done to her, they started to run away.

Morgan continued to lie on the ground for about five minutes, crying while she was touching her bruised face. She finally got up and started to walk back home, but as she was walking, her face felt as if was starting to repair all the bruises and swellings. When she noticed that her face was no longer hurting, she ran to a store window and saw her reflection, still crying hard. Her swollen face was no longer swollen and her lip healed instantly. When she saw that she had healed right before her eyes, she got the urge to turn back and head straight to college. She made it just in time, just before the college gate closed. Morgan entered the college and started to head into her first class. She sat right next to her bullies and stared at them to make them think that they were going crazy. After that day, she was never bullied again.

The rest of the family were much the same when it came to their feelings about not fitting in and feeling as if part of them did not belong on Earth. But they all tried very hard to block out their feelings and try to live normal lives.

On the 8th of September, Tami and her brother Harvey were talking about their futures and what their future holds. When they finally ended the conversation, Harvey told Tami that there would be a full moon that night.

Later that night, Tami's mother went into her room so they could have a conversation of their own. Mirian left when Tami fell asleep during the conversation, but Tami was not realising that she was having a dream within a dream, for she thought she was still up talking to her mother, when in fact she was actually sleeping.

As the night went on and was heading into the next morning, Tami heard a distressing scream coming from outside her patio doors. She woke up with a dreaded feeling and ran towards the patio doors with her unnerved body. She glanced down and saw a pale young woman frozen and in shock. Tami noticed that she was standing on the second step outside her studio flat rather than on the ground.

Then her eyes widened even more. When she saw thick white clouds slowly scurrying across the floor. She ran to get her mother to alert her about what was taking place and show her the astonishing discovery that was outside. Mirian went visibly numb, which led her to black out. Tami tried to awaken her mother, but she was still unconscious. Tami rushed downstairs to try to get Harvey to awaken her.

As soon as he heard Tami coming downstairs, he gazed into her eyes with amazement, and she knew that he saw the clouds that were on the floor. She headed to the front door, and as the door opened, the clouds slowly made its way inside the house. Harvey and Tami stepped outside, unable to believe what they were seeing. The sea was the sky, so the world appeared to be upside down. There were other people touching the clouds and playing with them. Everyone was clearly frightened yet amazed at the same time. Tami then went to feel the texture of the clouds and realized how cold they felt against her skin.

As Tami looked around her surroundings, she noticed that all the people had specific symbols on them. Some were wearing charm bracelets or protection signs, so she knew that they were special in some way. Tami abruptly paused and then turned to face a man directly. He seemed to be intently listening to a voice that was coming from a distance. She noticed that he was wearing a protection sign. The man started to shout, "We need to find a way to get up there. We were supposed to be up there, *not* down here!" The man was clearly starting to get impatient, as no one was paying him any attention or taking him seriously; they were plainly still astonished. Everyone started to look up to where clouds were supposed to be. But instead of the clouds being there, the sea was hovering over their heads. The people began looking at each other and asking that one question that was obviously sealed within them: "Is this real?" While the man to Tami's left was still shouting and trying to get his point across, she noticed something strange about the edge of the street pavement.

The pavement looked distant, as if it never ended. Tami walked up to the edge of the pavement. As she looked to the right to see how distant the pavement looked, her body felt injected with presentiment. Her eyes couldn't believe what they were seeing. In the distance, she saw herself—or someone who looked exactly like her. As Tami witnessed the unusual figure gazing at her, she quickly moved away. She felt tempted to have another look and to analyse the familiar figure. She had the courage to walk back and look straight down where the never-ending pavement was. Seeing the figure again, she was astounded to see that it was actually her. She moved her left hand up and started to do circular movements, and the figure that identified her started to imitate exactly what Tami was doing.

Tami wanted to have a closer look at her, so she moved towards her right, and as she was getting closer to herself, Tami soon realised that she was only couple of footsteps away. She began to take the smallest steps, and as she came eye-to-eye with herself, her heart felt as if it failed on her. She finally discovered that she was looking at *herself*! How was that even possible? She wondered as they were looking at each other. She had the courage to ask her who was she and what happened to the earth.

As Tami was asking the figure that looked like her the questions that she was dying to know the answers to, the other person's lips parted and she began to speak. It didn't sound like English, but Tami could still understand her. She introduced herself as Teekalla. Tami asked the lookalike figure where was she from, and Teekalla mentioned an unfamiliar name: Phenexus. She added that she was Tami's higher being. Teekalla explained to Tami that Phenexus was the planet where she was born, along with other beings. Tami was still amazed with what she was saying and where she said she was from. Teekalla added that Tami and her family had to find a way to get to her planet, but she didn't say what she needed to do or how it should be done. At this point, Tami got frustrated and confused because she didn't understand what she meant insofar as what she had to do.

She said in a soft voice that she had to go, but Tami was so eager to know more about what she was meant to do. Tami said desperately to Teekalla, "Please don't go," but Teekalla was walking off whilst the clouds were dancing and roaming around her, making it hard for to Tami to see her. She put out her hand to try to stop Teekalla from going, holding on to Teekalla's arm. Tami's hand felt as if it were wasting away, and as she looked to her left, she saw her hand holding Teekalla's arm.

Tami started to see her hand withering, slowly transforming an older hand. As Tami witnessed the transformation of her hand, she quickly pulled away from Teekalla's arm. When she did manage to take her hand away from what seemed to be some sort of blockage or barrier between them, Tami's hand went back to its original youthful skin. This was all too much for Tami to take in. Teekalla began to vanish, while Tami was standing there in amazement. She then turned back home to go tell Harvey what had happened to her and about the mission she had been given.

Heading towards her house, Tami saw Harvey, ran up to him, and started to explain what happened, how she saw her higher being from a planet called Phenexus. He looked at his sister, seeming unable to take it all in. So Tami left her brother outside, as he was still astonished with how the earth and atmosphere were changing. Once Tami reached her room, she sat on her bed and tried to make sense of the task that she had to do.

She started to think about the changes that were happening to the earth while hearing the man's desperate voice from outside shouting and encouraging the other residents to try to ascend like the rest to the unknown planet, which he was claiming was on top of the water, where the sky was meant to be. After the images and the voices in her head stopped, she glanced at the top of her wardrobe, where two large candles caught her attention. She took the two candles down and lit them, placed them on the floor, one to the left and one to the right side of her body. She started to close her eyes and clear her mind, as this allowed Tami to think of positive things that she had in her life as well as what she had done on Earth to help others.

Tami soon had the right mindset about staying positive and helping out others with a clear mind. Her subconscious mind was set free, and as her body became lighter, she knew deep down that she was no longer in her room. Tami's surroundings felt completely different. The smell was fresh and clean. Unfamiliar with her surroundings, she opened her eyes in amazement.

A man that was in the same room as Tami gave her a little introduction about their planet, telling her that

Phenexus was a lot like Earth. He said the beings on their planet were called Phenexians and lived much like humans, although they spoke a different language. They were also able to move around by levitating. Staring at the unique figure of a man, there was no doubt in her mind that she was no longer on Earth.

Tami looked around and discovered that she was in a massive room with white and black flooring and black and gold walls. The door in the room began to open. When it did, Tami saw herself again, her higher being. Her higher being said with an overwhelming voice, "You finally figured out how to get to planet Phenexus." As Tami's higher being was walking towards her, she realized that these beings had very different hair texture. Teekalla and the others had jet-black hair that resembled a calm waterfall, never seemed to end. Their hair needed to be swept back from their faces and tied up in a bun.

As for their skin colour and texture, it was unexplainable. It seemed as if the sun was reflecting on a mirror and the mirror was reflecting on their skin, giving them a unique golden colour, and their skin was absolutely clear and blemish-free. There were no lines such as the ones humans have that show the maturity of their skin. Tami was still in shock with what she discovered. She didn't have the ability to make sense of it all. Her mind became blank, which stopped her from reaching a reasonable conclusion.

As she started to walk towards her, Tami thought how beautiful she was. But Tami's thoughts drifted back to when everything did not seem so surreal. She felt that something was missing, but she didn't quite know what it was. As Teekalla began to talk to Tami, Tami suddenly remembered that her family was still on Earth.

Tami interrupted Teekalla, her higher being, telling her that she couldn't stay on Phenexus without her family. She asked if there was any way that she could contact her family, letting them know where she was and that she was safe. Tami stared into Teekalla's eyes and asked another question, whether her family would be able to join her on Phenexus. As she asked that nerve-racking question, Teekalla looked at her and said, "Orcaba", which meant *indeed*.

Tami asked her if she could use a telephone to call her family. Her higher self said in a light voice, "Follow me." Teekalla went outside the building, Tami following behind her. Tami thought to herself that the outside was even more beautiful than inside. It was filled with lots of flowers, and their sky had different shades of blues and oranges as well as deep red. This made for beautiful scenery because the clouds were big and fluffy, almost looking like the texture of thick candyfloss, giving the clouds a woven effect.

The fascinating colours that they had up there were indescribable to the eye. The colours on Phenexus would be unique down on Earth. According to Tami, everything was unique on Phenexus, including the ground they were walking on. It was like a clear crystal texture as they roamed along the floor.

Tami was still looking around, marvelling about how magnificent and beautiful Phenexus was. When she noticed her slowing down, Teekalla abruptly stopped to turn around. She touched her shoulders and stared into her worrying eyes, saying, "This is where you can contact your family." Tami began to look around her surroundings with confusion, for she only saw a beautiful fancy garden with a mini waterfall that looked like little crystals were flowing down it.

She noticed that there were no signs of any phone or physical object that she could use to contact her family. She asked Teekalla with confusion, "How am I supposed to contact my family if there's no sign of a technical gadget, like a phone or some sort of fax machine?"

Teekalla explained to her that there were no such things as phones or fax machines on Phenexus. She explained to Tami that the room they were in was called a connecture room. She continued by saying, "Whoever you feel like contacting, all you have to do is just think of the person and you will automatically get through to him or her." In order for this to work for Tami, she would need to have a clear and open mind.

Once Teekalla finished explaining what Tami would have to do in order to contact her family, Tami closed her eyes, took a deep breath, and started to take everything in by embracing the information that she was given. Once Tami knew what she had to do, she opened her eyes and started to walk closer to the little waterfall, Teekalla following a short distance behind her.

When the two got to the mini waterfall, Tami once again closed her eyes and began to think of her family. She started to see the strangest things, people that she hasn't seen before. She saw places that she didn't think even existed, and different colours started to appear. The colours were mystical to Tami because she had never seen colours like them before. Tami started to feel other emotions going through her and started to have different thoughts. Going through her mind, which gave her a strange feeling over her head, sort of like a signal. And when she decided to open her eyes, something incredible happened. She couldn't believe what was happening to her. Her body was still on Phenexus, but her spirit drifted on planet Earth, where her family was.

Tami felt like she was safely connected when she saw her mother walking around the house trying to find her. Tami saw her mother and screamed her name out from the top of her lungs. Mirian heard the desperate call from her daughter. She stopped what she was doing and called out Tami's name, asking her where she was. Tami replied, and her mother was looking around with amazement on her face whilst she was still talking to Tami. Mirian asked how she could hear her daughter and not see her. Tami figured that the only way to make her mother understand was to tell her exactly what happened to her and what she had to do in order to get up to planet Phenexus.

She started to explain to her mother what she had to do, which was to gather the rest of the family and to create a circle with two candles placed on the floor. By the time Tami had explained in detail what they needed to do, her body started to weaken, which was a sign that her spirit had to go back into her body. Tami began to lose focus and control over her words, as her spirit had to get back to her body on Phenexus.

Once her mother gathered the specialty candles that she needed, she then called to the others and had them gather in a circle in the same room, each of them sitting down next to the candles that were placed around them.

Tami opened her eyes and felt the connection between her family because the circle felt very strong. Teekalla spoke to Tami and told her that she could still manage to connect to her family as they created a tight circle. Tami began to stare into Teekalla's eyes and managed to speak to her mother through her mind. Tami connected with her mother and told her to close her eyes as well as have everyone in the room do so. As her mother told the others in the room to close their eyes, her brother Harvey just vanished into thin air and managed to reach Phenexus successfully.

Tanarla closed her eyes and started to laugh and giggle, and this made her vanish as well. Because she was thinking happy and positive thoughts, Tanarla managed to succeed and joined Tami and Harvey. As Tanarla ascended into Phenexus, she had a breathtaking experience. When Tanarla saw someone that looked exactly like her, she quickly ran towards herself and gave herself a massive hug. Talisha watched as the others started disappearing one by one, leading the room to be quiet and tense.

Soon only Michael, Talisha, and Mirian – as well as Jade, their cat – were left. Once Michael realised that two of his siblings had succeeded, he started to focus hard. By closing his eyes and thinking about the good that he had done on Earth, he vanished also. As she realised that nearly everyone was gone, Talisha began to cry and tremble because she started to feel the pressure.

Her mother took her hands and held them close to her chest, telling her to look directly into her eyes. And as she slowly looked into her mother's eyes, Mirian started to talk about their funny moments they had with each other and the times that they helped each other out. Doing this gave them the right connection and belief to join everyone else on planet Phenexus. They brought the cat with them also, as the cat was sitting in the middle of them. This gave them enough power and energy to bring him along.

When they ascended, they saw themselves in a completely new world. They almost felt as if they had been given a second chance in life. Teekalla and the rest met up with Mirian and Talisha outside the Phenexus kingdom. There was a giant statue form resting on a huge golden clear and black throne. They were all lost for words as they looked up and saw the magnificent figure sitting on a humungous throne. Everyone started to take small steps back to get a better view. Suddenly, the statue figure began to move its head and hands in what seemed like slow motion.

This was a very scary experience for Tami as well as her family. Teekalla started to laugh at their reaction towards the moving statue, which happened to be the king and the protector of Phenexus.

They were all eager to know about the mysterious statue and its purpose. But Mirian realised that two of her other daughters had not ascended to where they were. She gently tapped Teekalla's shoulders and asked her if her daughters could join her and rest on Phenexus. Teekalla looked at Mirian with her innocent eyes and promised Mirian that they were working on a way to get Fiona and Morgan to ascend.

Teekalla saw one of the Phenexians heading into one of the buildings. She ran towards her and whispered into her ears. The female Phenexian looked over to where Mirian and her family were standing and quickly rushed into the building. Everyone looked at each other with confusion because they couldn't quite make out what Teekalla was saying to the other Phenexian. Minutes went by and Teekalla was making everyone nervous because she kept looking up in the sky as if waiting for something to fall out of the sky. Harvey asked Teekalla if she needed to tell them anything.

A tall and wide figure called out Teekalla's name from a distance, asking her to come, as well as Mirian and her family. Teekalla smiled when she told them to follow her into the building. As they approached the male figure, they were calling out Teekalla's name from a distance. As they got closer to the male Phenexian, they saw that he had long, thick hair. He introduced himself as Exstronis and began to explain that he was someone else's higher being who ascended from Earth.

Everyone started to analyse and examine Exstronis's appearance and style. Teekalla whispered into Exstronis's ears. She told Mirian and the rest to wait where they were standing until she returned.

Teekalla began to run behind Exstronis and headed straight into one of the closed doors. Minutes started to stroll by, making it feel like hours. The doors started to open when they saw Teekalla and Exstronis heading out of the room with two old women who had some sort of sliver blanket around them. Michael, being the youngest, disobeyed Teekalla's order and left the spot that he was told not to move from. Mirian reached out her arm to try to grab him back towards her. But it was too late. Michael had already sped off in the direction of Teekalla. But Michael immediately slowed down his pace when he realised that the two old women that he saw with his family were actually Morgan and Fiona. He was traumatised when he saw his two sisters in that state.

He turned around, headed straight to his mother, and started to cry. Mirian ran towards Michael and asked him what happened, what he had seen. But before he had pulled himself together and taken a deep breath, Teekalla hovered to where Mirian and her kids were standing, informing them that although Fiona and Morgan ascended, a few complications occurred. Mirian's heart sank when she was listening to what Teekalla was telling her. But Exstronis interrupted what Teekalla was saying and told Mirian that everything would be just fine. Mirian looked at the rest of her kids and smiled.

Teekalla gave a positive impression that she had everything under control, which made Mirian and the rest feel much better. Teekalla turned to Exstronis and told him to take them into the recovery room. Exstronis did exactly that, hovering Fiona's and Morgan's bodies into the air and heading them straight into another building where the recovery room was based. Teekalla started to explain what normally happened inside the recovery room and how people from Earth who ascended with complications would need to go straight into the recovery rooms. But before Teekalla finished her sentence, they heard three voices, one male and two females.

When Teekalla looked to her left, she noticed three friends coming towards: Alexius, Gerrainea, and Brotacus.

They had animated smiles on their faces. When they got closer to Teekalla and the rest, they introduced themselves. Brotacus said in a deep bass voice, "Welcome to the planet Phenexus." Brotacus was 180 years old, and he was widely built and had the strength of eight men. He was smart as well as funny and gentle. But Brotacus had a serious side to him which he wasn't proud of, but because he was in charge of the most serious decisions, it took his mind off the hidden anger that he did not quite understand.

Alexius was 150 years old and was a powerful warrior. She was very fierce and fast on her feet but petite in size. But that did not stop her from being one of the greatest warriors of all time.

Gerrainea, who was 180 years old, was Teekalla's closest friend and had the ability to sense people's emotions and read their thoughts. She also had the special gift of manipulating her opponents. She was humble and funny, never taking life too seriously. But her true ability was never needed, as Phenexus was a peaceful and loving planet. The only time she really needed to use her gift was when their planet aligned with XSoraya, which was another parallel planet to theirs. But that day was never to be spoken of.

When Teekalla's three friends finished introducing themselves, they said at the same time with excitement, "We would love to show you around Phenexus and to educate you about the statue figure that you see before you." By the time Teekalla's friends finished what they had to say, everyone was delighted and excited to have the opportunity to understand what Phenexus was all about. As well as the people there, Tami and her family agreed to have a tour of Phenexus.

Teekalla and her friends started to walk behind the massive tree from behind the gigantic statue. They began to break the branches off the trees, which were full of leaves, and then headed towards Tami's family. They started to give everyone the individual branches to hold, saying to them, "You will all need to eat five individual leaves in order for the magic to happen."

Everyone, including Mirian, picked off five individual leafs and started to eat them one by one.

Alexius told Tanarla and the rest to close their eyes and to imagine their favourite foods. Out of nowhere, Tami, Michael, and Harvey began to scream aloud because they started to taste their favourite foods, such as fish, chicken, chocolate, pasta, and so forth. Their reactions attracted the rest of their family's attention. They started to do the same, closing their eyes and thinking about their favourite foods.

Once they were satisfied from the different tastes of their favourite foods, they started to feel extremely light, as if they were hovering in thin air. They all slowly opened their eyes after eating the last leaf and noticed that they were no longer on the ground. The feeling for the others was sensational, for they saw themselves hovering over Phenexus buildings as well as the Phenexian beings.

Gerrainea started to show them the buildings as well as what they represented. Brotacus and Alexius educated the Hall family about how each individual Phenexian being had his own unique identity. Each identity was shown by the unique pattern displayed on the side of his face.

They were able to see the majority of Phenexus and the beautiful landscape of the unique buildings as well as the beautiful beings that lived there: the Phenexians. They still were eager to know more about the great figure of a man sitting outside his kingdom in the open air. As they all approached the giant statue and began to hover around it, they all noticed that the statue figure was watching over this magnificent planet. Eventually, the unique statue began to move its head and hands with a slow motion.

Teekalla said with excitement, "It's my turn to teach them something!" She started to lead them to the statue. She told the Hall family that the statue was actually a person called King Exous, from their planet. "King Exous guides and protects us from danger. He also warns us when the next planet alignment will be. That's why the king has to be sitting outside with his throne."

The king stood up and glanced down to where Tami and her family were standing. As this oversized figure smiled, he left his throne and started walking towards them. Then the weirdest thing happened. As King Exous began to walk towards Mirian's family, he started to shrink and become a normal size. King Exous started to get closer to the family. Jade, the family cat, jumped out of Mirian's hands and started to run towards the king. Everyone noticed that the king reached into his pocket and pulled out a little crown.

Jade noticed the crown and jumped into king Exous's arms, starting to lick his face. The king placed a miniature crown on Jade's head and began to stroke his back. Jade turned around to look at Tami and winked at her, starting to purr at the king. The king later said to Jade with a passionate voice, "Well done. Good job."

Tami started to have a good look at the king from the throne. While the king was walking slowly towards them. Tami started to yell at the top of her voice, saying, "You can't take my cat away from me. That's my cat, not yours!"

While Tami was yelling at the king with frustration she got the king's full attention, when she heard everyone stop talking. She slowly stopped to look around and noticed that everyone was looking at her.

The king answered her with a gentle voice as he started to explain who Jade really was. He began by explaining that Jade was sent down to earth to lead them on the right path and to keep her family safe. The king added that Jade was his right-hand protector, Jade looked into Tami's eyes and licked her hand. As she began to slowly stroke her cat's back, she slowly looked up to where the king was standing and asked him what was his main purpose. King Exous touched her shoulders and said, 'I am the protector of this wonderful planet.' Tami smiled at the king as he began to walk towards his throne with Jade. Everyone noticed that the king and Jade increased in size, as the king sat down on his throne beside jade.

Tami and the rest were looking at one another with amazement. Teekalla said with a soft voice, 'It's time to explore the rest of Phenexus.'

While Teekalla was getting ready to show some areas of her planet, Harvey noticed that while they were walking, they were hovering over the ground, but he could still see his footprints on the floor. Teekalla started to show the Hall family the rest of the amazing and unique areas of Phenexus.

Brotacus and Alexius did not get to finish off showing them the rest of Phenexus due to the excitement and fascination that they had towards the king. But the majority of the parts that Teekalla showed them were absolutely beautiful and breathtaking. The colours were almost surreal; for instance, their grass was an out-of-this-world strong green colour. Their flowers had little and big crystals on them.

Teekalla and her close friends then led them into a beautiful garden. While they were walking into the garden, they sat down and were accompanied by some usual creatures.

The animals on Phenexus weren't the particular animals known to be on Earth. The unrealistic animals on planet Earth that were normally portrayed as being fairy tales were actually real. They saw mermaids, unicorns, fairies, and other unique animals that could not be identified. The unique animals that they saw had suede skin, with clear glass eyes and no pupils in sight. The more they passed the unique creatures, the more they started to realise the different size and shapes.

As they were sitting on the fresh green grass, they noticed butterflies but with more wings on their backs, designed with significant symbols on each side of the wings. Michael saw a massive lake nearby and started to walk towards it.

When he got closer to it, he saw goldfish the size of massive sharks.

Tanarla saw something moving behind the trees, and she decided to get up from where she was sitting and check it out. When she got closer to the tree, she saw a half man, half horse hiding behind a tree, and when she saw this unusual creature/human, she started to run away from it. But with a soft voice the half man, half horse said, “Please don’t be afraid. I wouldn’t harm you.”

Tanarla suddenly stopped and turned her head to where the half man, half horse was standing. She asked him in a shaky voice. “What happened to you? Why do you look like that?”

The half man half horse came out from behind the tree and replied, “I’m what they would call a centaur.” He began to say that in Tanarla’s world, his kind would normally be advertised as a myth, but on planet Phenexus, anything was possible. As the centaur was still talking, Tanarla walked around him and started to touch his tail and legs. The centaur asked Tanarla what her name was and asked if she knew about the truth.

“My name is Tanarla, and it’s a pleasure to meet you.” But then she realised what the centaur said after that, about her knowing the truth, and she looked at him with a strong focus. “What truth?” she asked him. The centaur froze for about ten seconds, and Tanarla had to say, “Hello, is anyone there?”

The centaur slowly came out of his trance and started to analyse his surroundings, saying the word

"Antarocx." As he said his name, he began to run but did not look back from where they were standing.

When Antarocx left, Tanarla felt unsettled, as she didn't quite know what he wanted to tell her. But as she looked around, she saw her family happy and free. She didn't really want to ruin things, so Tanarla decided to put it behind her. With a smile on her face, she rushed to where everyone was sitting. As she was running, she saw some beautiful birds with unique colours flying around her.

The others were at peace because they were relaxed and calm. The clouds in the sky looked so thick. But something appeared in the candyfloss texture clouds from a distance. When their vision started to become clearer, everyone witnessed what seemed to be a silver flying horse known on Earth as Pegasus. Unable to believe her eyes, Talisha began to rub them.

To make sure her eyes weren't playing tricks on her, she got up from where she was lying down. The flying horse was heading straight towards them. Talisha started to jump and waved her hands in the air so the flying horse would know exactly where to land. As the flying horse known as Pegasus on Earth landed in the garden on the fresh green grass, everyone started to walk behind Talisha. The flying horse started to approach the Hall family. Teekalla, Talisha, and her friends reached out her hand so they could stroke the beautiful creature that was standing before them. She noticed that the colours of the flying horse started to change to different shades of silver whenever anyone touched parts of its body.

Brotacus said, "Don't worry. All our creatures on planet Phenexus are absolutely harmless. And to prove it, who would like to ride Flyars?"

Harvey said with confusion, "I'm guessing that's the flying horse's name, right?"

The others began to laugh and raise their hands, as they were truly excited to ride a real Pegasus. Brotacus looked at Michael and pointed at him so he could be the first to ride. Mirian was a little bit unsettled with his choice because Michael was the youngest there. But Mirian brushed it off when she saw how beautiful and peaceful Phenexus really was.

Brotacus placed Michael on a stool because Flyars was enormous. He told him to look into Flyars's eyes and see if he could create at least one tear from an eye. He turned his face to Brotacus and asked him why. Teekalla jumped in and said that is how to let Flyars know that he could trust you. As it made sense to Michael, he started to look into Flyars's eyes. And when he did, little droplets of diamonds started to come out from the horse's eyes. This made his eyes tear up, knowing he had successfully done what he had to do in order for Flyars to trust him. He moved the stool and placed it where he would need to jump to get on his back. Flyars wings began to flap up and down. As the force was so strong, Mirian and her family had to hold their breaths. And with a blink of an eye, they saw Michael flying in the beautiful sky. After that, everyone had a turn riding on Flyars, which was a sensational feeling for everyone.

After that amazing experience of actually having the opportunity to fly in the sky and touch the soft fluffy clouds, a young woman called from a distance, saying, "It's time to have abroo." Teekalla told them that it was the equivalent of food on Earth.

Tami said underneath her breath, "Why don't they just call it food?" Mirian pinched Tami and told her not to be rude. Teekalla looked at Tami and winked her eye. Alexius and Brotacus led them to where the woman had called them, which was around the corner from a garden that was full of weird-looking foods.

One of the Phenexians walked up to the family, introduced herself as Exstara, and began handing out the strange food. Mirian was apprehensive about tasting the food. She didn't want to be disrespectful or rude, so she said that she had a sensitive tummy and didn't want to taste it and fall sick.

Tami told her brother to have a taste, and by the expression on his face, she could see that he was quite surprised at how unique the food tasted. They all decided to tuck in and enjoy the unique food that they were given. The different tastes that were rushing through their mouths were unexplainable.

Teekalla had other Phenexians helping her. One of them rushed to a waterfall similar to the one where Tami was escorted so she could contact her family. But this waterfall that the Phenexian ran towards was a place to collect water in what seemed to be an invisible jug. There were different shapes and sizes of rocks imbedded beside the beautiful waterfall. Tami also identified sparkling diamonds and crystals actually placed into the rocks. The Phenexian began to collect the diamonds and put them in the jug, serving as ice because they were so cold. The water that was in the invisible jug changed into what seemed to be a deep red wine colour. He brought the jug back to them and placed it on the fresh green grass, and then he returned to the waterfall.

There was a river right next to it, and he buried his hand in the water and collected something from it. It looked like fish, and he presented it on a fancy plate. They each had a taste of the odd-looking fish, and surprisingly it tasted like well-seasoned chicken.

On the side of the plate was also what looked like green leaves. But once again, they weren't what they seemed to be. They tasted like prawn noodles. They were absolutely divine. He went away and came back with another tray, which held something that had been grated finely. It melted in their mouths and tasted like caramel and apple pie. Mirian was satisfied with the unique food that she received.

After eating, they all decided to have a well-earned rest. They were thinking how wonderful and blessed they were to have the opportunity to ascend into Phenexus.

When they woke up the next morning, Teekalla called for Tami and the others to meet her downstairs. They headed out of the rooms, which were next to each other, and went downstairs. They saw the king standing next to her. He explained to them that they would be doing something that morning that involved their fears. With no answers or questions, the king called out Tami's name first. She followed Teekalla as she was taken into a room called the fear-learn-conquer station. Teekalla told her that the fear-learn-conquer training station was designed to conquer fears. As Tami was listening to what Teekalla was saying, her body started to shake. She knew what the training station had in store for her.

Her higher being, Teekalla, added that once you step foot in the fear-learn-conquer room, it would pick up on one of your main fears and use it against you. She told Tami that she would need to use all her energy and thoughts. "You will need to find a way to control the training room, not let the training room control you."

When Tami was in the training station, she heard a voice start to speak robotically. "Tami, you have an anxiety disorder." She heard the two words that she had been running away from for so many years. She started to run towards the door. But by the time she got there, the door disappeared, as well as the robotic voice. She turned around and noticed that she was trapped in a large football stadium before a huge crowd, which made it worse for Tami. She was right at the top of the stadium, where people were shouting and pushing each other. Tami's heart started to beat faster, which caused her to sweat. She thought that she was going to have a heart attack. So she quickly ran towards the exit doors, hoping that they would open. But they didn't.

Within the blink of an eye, Tami knew what she had to do. She had to make it down to the bottom of the stadium. She went down the steep stairs without holding on to the bars. She then realised how close she was to the ground. Tami started to dance down the stairs like it was her graduation day. She couldn't believe how free she felt after walking down the stairs full of people. By the time Tami reached the bottom of the step, she realised that she was back in the training station. She could see her family standing outside with their arms open.

When it was Michael's turn to go in, he looked behind him. He saw his family standing there trying to convince him that there was nothing to worry about. So Michael had enough courage to enter the training station room. He waved at his family and said, "I'll be back in few minutes." As the doors were slowly closing in on each other, the fear-learn-conquer session started. The same robotic voice that Tami heard started to talk to Michael.

"You have something called coulrophobia." Michael had tears coming from his eyes because he knew what to expect. The robotic voice told Michael to close his eyes for ten seconds and then to open them. When he opened one eye, he realised that he was no longer in the training station. He was in a dusty old bedroom with no light in sight, but strangely, a spotlight appeared in the middle of the bedroom and shined on a big rocking chair where a clown appeared from nowhere. With a disturbing smile on its face, it began to rock back and forth on the big rocking chair, its arms reaching out to grab Michael. As Michael began to look away from where the clown was rocking, mirrors started to appear everywhere, sort of like a house of mirrors. It gave Michael the illusion that no matter where he looked, he would see the clown.

Michael walked up to the mirrors and broke every single one of them by hitting them with a pole that was near the rocking chair. He began to feel excitement and joy, when he looked at the clown, he realised that the smile that was on the clown's face had turned into a frown. He said, "I am no longer afraid of you. You are nothing to me now I overpower you."

When Michael said those confident words, his training session was over. The robotic voice opened the doors for Michael, and that's when he saw his family waiting outside the room to congratulate him for his success on conquering his fears.

After everyone gave Michael a hug to congratulate him, he tapped Tanarla's hand and told her that she was up next. She accepted what she had to do, as she started to walk closer to the station to conquer her fears. She decided not to look back at where her family were standing because it would have made her too emotional and nervous to go in. She managed to step into the training station, the doors slowly closed behind her. She heard a robotic voice telling her to close her eyes and take a deep breath. When Tanarla closed her eyes, she realised that she was sitting down holding a steering wheel. She quickly opened her eyes and saw a little girl crossing the road. But as she slammed on her brakes, she realised that the brakes and the clutch had been tampered with.

It was too late to do anything, and the car hit the little girl. Tanarla rushed out of the car feeling light-headed. She hurried to check on the little girl, but she was nowhere to be found. Tanarla got back into the car and closed her eyes, and began to cry. But the weirdest thing happened to her. She realised that the car was moving. Her hands were still on the steering wheel when the same girl that she hit crossed the same road. Tanarla started to push down on her brakes. But once again the brakes were tampered with. She hurried out of the car, to check on the little girl to see if she was ok and mysteriously the little girl vanished. This happened to Tanarla three times. She decided to go to another route in order to try avoiding going down the same road where she kept hitting the little girl.

Tanarla continued to drive down what seemed to be a never-ending road. When she was coming close to a sign, she couldn't really figure out what the sign was saying. But when she got closer to it, she realised that she was heading to the edge of a cliff. When she saw the sign she quickly opened the car door and rolled out. The car went straight down the cliff, causing a massive explosion. She opened her eyes which were full of tears, and realised that she was back in the training station. Her session had finished. She thought to herself that she must have had an accelerated probability power because she was able to see herself in different angles, which allowed her to pick the best option for her to escape the situation that she was put in. This allowed her to predict the outcomes of the choices she made. But she pushed her thoughts to the side and ran out of the training room station, wiping her tears away.

It was Talisha's turn when her higher being, Diamond, escorted her to the training room station. She whispered in her ear and told her to focus on what could help her escape the situation. Talisha looked at Diamond with confusion because she didn't really pick up on what she was saying. Talisha was about to ask Diamond to repeat what she'd said but it was too late. The station doors began to open, and her hands started to sweat and shake. When Diamond left her standing outside the doors, she took a deep breath and began to walk inside. She saw a chair located in the middle of the room, and when the same robotic voice told her to take a seat and to wait for instructions, she went to the chair and sat down. She had to wait five minutes until she heard the robotic voice telling her that she had a fear of rejection. Talisha couldn't believe what she heard; she'd never spoken about her fear to anyone. The robotic voice continued to tell her that she would need to complete a task. All Talisha had to do was to get a key from the corner of the room and open the door of the training station.

It seemed straightforward to Talisha, but she had a strange feeling about this. When it was time for her task to start, she got up from where she was sitting and headed straight towards the key, managing to take it down from the corner of the room. She opened the station door.

Talisha couldn't believe how quickly she accomplished her task. She was overwhelmed when she saw her family waiting outside the door for her. She ran to them and gave them a group hug, tears starting to roll down her face. But her family abruptly pushed her away from them and started to shout out negative things about her. Talisha was confused about why her family was acting like that towards her. She looked at everyone and asked them to stop acting so negative.

Mirian told Talisha to shut up. "I can't stand the sight of you!" she exclaimed.

Michael then told Talisha that she would never amount to anything.

Talisha burst into tears. Listening to her family was making her feel worthless.

Tami made her way to the front and punched Talisha in the face, telling her to shut up and go away. As Talisha started covering the eye that Tami had punched, she remembered what her higher being said whilst whispering in her ear. So she gathered enough courage and started to defend herself. She noticed that their eyes started to cry black ink-like tears. Slowly but surely, she saw them evaporate into little specks of dust.

When she closed her eyes and opened them again, she realised that she was still sitting on the chair. She noticed that the key was still in the corner of the room. Talisha didn't know what to think, whether it was her mind playing tricks on her. Or was it true what the robotic voice told her, that her training was finished?

She made her way to the doors. As the doors opened, she saw her family waiting outside for her. She took baby steps towards them and asked them, "Are you guys yourselves now?"

Mirian replied, "What are you talking about?" As Talisha heard those words, she knew that everything was a figment of her imagination. She began to run towards her family and gave every single one of them a hug and a kiss, telling them how much she loved them.

Harvey's higher being, Skyian, whispered in his ear and told him that he would need to go to the station room so he could do his task. Harvey went and told his family that he was up next and they all followed him to the training station and gave him hugs of encouragement. When it was Tami's turn to hug her brother, she also whispered in his ears to inform him about the robotic voice and how he should pay close attention to what the voice is telling him to do.

Harvey hugged his sister and left his family whilst he was entering the training station. He noticed a blindfold lying on the floor. As he began to walk further inside, the doors began to close. He heard the same robotic voice that Tami was telling him about. The voice had far surpassed Harvey's anticipation; he expected a normal digitalized voice, which did not have any sense of life. He felt a severe case of rubatosis. His heartbeats were irregular, his pulsations increased with great force.

If there were a continuance of incorrect breathing, his cardiovascular system would shut down with no sign of hesitation. The intense sensation wrapping down his spine slowly reaching to his bladder, which he felt was filled to the brim. Waiting to be excreted silently. Hoping to cool down his temperature; the feelings a figment of his imagination, the emotions triggered by his instructions. The voice asking him to pick up the blindfold and put it on. Harvey obeyed and covered his eyes. After one minute, the robotic voice told him to take of the blindfold.

When he removed the blindfold, Harvey was terrified and confused because he was no longer in the training station; he was actually in a small and cramped house standing in a hallway. Harvey started to feel claustrophobic. He felt like the walls were closing in on him, the air getting thin. His vision began to weaken. He wondered how long it would be before the oxygen supply was depleted. Harvey started to look around and headed towards the kitchen for any water in sight.

As Harvey was looking for water, he also was trying to find a way out. Every door he went through, he ended up in the same hallway where he'd started. He squinted to see if there was an ending to the corridor. His eyes could not quite pinpoint the end of the hallway. Minimising the gravity around his feet caused him to levitate, and he was overwhelmed by the phenomenon. But he knew he could not be too shocked. That could cause him to break a solidifying focus, and he was aware that constantly walking would deplete his energy, also causing a need for energy resources for rejuvenation. Hovering down the stairs gave him a vibrational sensation which automatically caused him to scrunch his toes.

After becoming familiarised with the vibration, he made his way to the kitchen, which had no furniture but had a refrigerator. Harvey lessened the gravity around the fridge, causing it to rise inches from the floor, leaving nothing but the shadows drowning in the cracks of the wood. He opened the freezer door and gazed at the blocks of ice. Harvey said, "Somehow I have to create enough water to lubricate the dry air." Harvey scraped all the ice and broke all the icicles that he could.

Gathering all the ice and telekinetically rubbing all the pieces together caused friction among the ice, creating water that rose inches from the ceiling. It made the air moist, and Harvey managed to manipulate the water, turning it into a box-like shape that was mobile.

Everywhere Harvey went, the container followed him as his oxygen supply. Harvey had two agendas: first was to create an oxygen supply; the second was to escape from the never-ending house. He levitated to the hallway with the uncountable doors, as his mind was not occupied with trying to find oxygen. His mind was able to roam freely. But his mind started to fixate on doors leading to the same hallway. There were no windows, just a sense of entrapment.

This caused a high volume of sweating and dizziness, but Harvey used the symptoms of his fear as motivation to decrease more gravity around his feet. Protruding his head forward, he flew at an unfathomable speed to see how far the hallway went. He projected down the hallway for three or four minutes, hoping to get a stroke of good luck. He closed his eyes as he was flying; he knew it was safe travelling in the same direction as long as he did not turn left or right. The hallway was narrow, and his intuition told him to stop flying, to relax, and to take deep breaths. As his inner voice spoke, it resonated with him and he stopped immediately. He closed his eyes and took seven deep breaths from his diaphragm. He felt that he was one with nature. He felt more receptive, relaxed, and blissful.

Opening one of the doors, he saw that the door handle was gold-plated and rather warm. The door and frame had slight cracks and felt frail. Walking through the door with his eyes closed, he felt a gush of air brush between his fingers. Opening his eyes, he saw that he was back at the training station with his hands in the same shape the door handle was in. The only difference was that he was holding nothing. The training room station doors opened slowly, catching Harvey's attention. He ran to the open door and emerged with a big smile on his face. He felt as if he'd conquered his greatest challenge in life. His mother ran up to him and gave him a big hug. Mirian's higher being, Indigo, touched her shoulder and told her that she was up next. Indigo took her to the training room station and opened the door for her. Mirian's heart started to beat faster, as different thoughts were going through her mind. Mirian entered the training room, the same digitalized voice told her to take a seat. After two minutes passed, the voice told Mirian to close her eyes and take a deep breath. Suddenly she felt like her body was floating in the air, meaning she was negating gravity. As she slowly opened her eyes, she noticed that she was no longer in the training station. She began to see a maze appear right before her very eyes. Mirian entered the maze that was of vast dull colours. Making her feel physically sick, she took a gasp of air and pulled herself together. She continued to walk straight ahead; when she came across a barricade of throne flowers. She had no other choice but to turn back on herself. And go towards another direction, when she came across a young child with a luminescent halo surrounding her. The little girl had black hair with silver streaks, but her face was not identified as Mirian could only see her back. Although the little girl's back was facing Mirian, the young girl was able to raise her left hand and point straight ahead. She began to follow in the girl's direction. When she realised that the little girl's feet were not on the ground. She was actually hovering as she was turning corners. Mirian realised that the colouring around the little girl had changed from electric blue to a fiery red and a sunshine of warm yellow. The colours displayed around the girl represented the colours of danger, caution and safety. With no communication between them; Mirian was intrigued to find out what the little girl looked like. But her curiosity was satisfied when the little girl stopped abruptly to turn around. Mirian was shocked by the features that appeared back at her. She was looking at a mirror image of herself.

The girl opened her mouth and said four words: “I am your instincts!”

“How did you materialise?” Mirian asked.

“I am projection of your subconscious,” the girl replied.

Mirian was cogitating and came up with a conclusion, that the colours emanating from the little girl were actually Mirian's own emotions. The little girl held Mirian’s hand and was able to look directly into her eyes. This allowed Mirian to see a nanosecond of the future.

At that point, Mirian knew exactly what to do in order to get out of the maze. The little girl vanished, Mirian quickly started to walk to the direction where she had to go. From nowhere a light appeared and she began to follow it. Suddenly the light took on the shape of a human figure. The human figure pointed to the door and she opened the door with a force that she never knew she had.

She felt such relief and felt so free. She was happy that she had conquered her fear and made it through the training. As she opened the door and walked outside, her supportive family was there waiting for her. Tears started to roll down Mirian’s face, and she rushed to her kids and gave each and every one of them a big hug. She stared into her children’s eyes and said, “Fear can only conquer you if you allow it to.”

After they had all conquered their fears, King Exous opened the main doors and congratulated them all on their success. The king then paused and looked at everyone. He said, "Tomorrow is the real test for everyone." He immediately focused on Fiona and Morgan because they'd missed the first part of the training due to the late ascendance.

Harvey said in a hostile voice, "Why do we need to do another test? We all passed the test for the training station." Harvey added that it was irrelevant.

The king focused on Harvey and gave him a cheeky smirk. King Exous replied, "We are doing this so all of you can see your true potential." The others were dead silent, not quite understanding what the king meant.

Princess Valentani, the king's daughter, blinked her eyes three times to notify the rest of the higher beings to take the Hall family to their rooms so they could luxuriate and recharge. Skyian and Izion led the way. When they all started to head out of the room, Tami looked over her shoulder. She saw the king shaking his head with disappointment as he was walking towards Princess Valentani.

Tami knew that something was wrong, and she told Teekalla that she needed to go back into the room that they were in because she'd left something in there. Tami had seen an opportunity to find out the real reason that she and her family were chosen to ascend into Phenexus. Teekalla told her to go get it and meet her straight after that. Tami began to follow the king and princess into another room.

When King Exous looked at his daughter and began to speak about Tami's family, he sounded concerned about the family not being able to believe in themselves. Different thoughts started to fly around in Tami's mind. She did not quite understand why it was so important for her family to believe in themselves and for the king to approve it. While Tami was still trying to work out what the king was up to, King Exous continued to talk about how he felt about her family.

But before the king managed to finish of his sentences, Tami heard Teekalla calling out her name from a distance, which startled her. She got up from where she was hiding and ran straight towards the sound of Teekalla's voice. Tami saw Teekalla from a distance, tapping her feet and looking impatient, but when she approached, Teekalla she simply told Tami to go to her resting room. Then she said, "I want you to get enough rest and energy for tomorrow's last and important training station."

The next day, all the higher beings started to wake everyone up before sun rise. Heading out of their rooms, they saw the king standing outside the hallway holding a big grey key in his left hand. The awkward silence was disrupted by Harvey's voice when he said three confident words: "We are ready." King Exous looked at Harvey and then looked at his higher being, Skyian, and told him to get the room ready.

Mirian looked behind her and hugged her kids, saying in a low voice, "Everything and everyone will be just fine." When she turned her head to look at the king with doubt, the rest of the higher beings that were outside waiting until the training rooms was ready to be in use. Skyian walked up to the king and began to whisper into his ears. This made Morgan and the rest more anxious to know what was going and what was being said. King Exous left the higher beings from where they were standing and walked up to Tami and the rest to have a heart-to-heart talk.

As everyone listened to the king's uneasy voice telling them that they must take the last training session seriously because their lives depended on it, King Exous looked at Mirian and her family. When he saw the fear in their eyes, the king cleared his throat and started to explain that the training session did not have to be long or hard if they all stuck together and supported each other at all times.

Michael put his hands on his face. He then spoke in a brittle voice, almost sounding as if he were about to cry. "I don't want to do this whole process of the training session anymore."

Mirian placed Michael's head against her chest and told him to listen to the king's words, assuring him that everything would be OK if he just believed and worked together as a team.

Brotacus informed the king that the final training station was ready for use. The king lifted his head up high and told Mirian and her kids to follow Brotacus. They did so and found that the training station was mysteriously built away from the other training stations.

Walking closer to the doors, Tami realised that there were some sort of unique description above them. Morgan and Fiona turned to their higher beings, Skylar and Millik, to ask them what the description meant.

Millik said, "The description you see before you was carved one thousand years ago by a being called Peradoox.

He was the protector of Phenexus before King Exous." As Millik was getting deep into the explanation, Skylar pinched Millik's arm and whispered something in her ear, which led Millik to walk away from where they were standing. Brotacus rushed around the corner once again to tell the king that the training stations were ready.

They gathered everyone in a circle and touched each of their foreheads. A unique symbol appeared on top of each person's forehead. The king told them that the symbol was for protection and other uses, but it was up to them to find out how it worked. King Exous and the higher beings began to walk, and Mirian and the rest strolled behind. They headed outside and saw a massive door that stood alone. The king stopped to insert the grey key that he was still carrying. The King took a deep breath and asked everyone to be prepared for when the doors opened. As they approached the door, mysteriously their clothes changed into distinctive uniforms that had special effects and displayed the sky. Thunder and lightning were calmly moving around the uniform. They were all astonished with their new outfits.

This was all too surreal for Fiona and Morgan. Once they pulled themselves together, they felt ready to take on the challenge. The king slowly started to turn the key that was placed in the keyhole. There was a click. Izion and Indigo headed out to the training area and came back with what seemed to be a glowing white tube. Out of curiosity, Morgan asked Indigo, “What’s that weird-looking object you’re holding in your hand?”

The king increased in size as if he was threatened by something. He said in a deep voice, “It’s called a turbojector. It’s the memory from the fear-learn-conquer room. It managed to pick up on all your fears and rapid moves. Then it gathers them all together and releases them out into this specific station door.”

After they heard the king’s unsettling words, they all held hands and crept into the training station. A loud bang echoed behind them, and they all realised that the door had sealed itself. Their unique clothing started to change effects and colours.

The ground started to shake, and little cracks on the ground started to appear. And out of those cracks came out big snakes that was of a slivery colour. Out of nowhere, buildings started to appear, and people were walking up and down the streets. Morgan and Fiona felt as if their hearts were going to pound out of their chests.

They all stood in a straight line, side by side, looking around at what almost seemed to be Earth. But Harvey thought to himself that they couldn’t be on Earth because they’d only entered the training station. Harvey stared to repeat the words, “It’s only a test; it’s only a test.”

Then the test began. When unidentified objects came out from the sky, creating miniature fireballs, Tami and the rest ran towards what seemed to be an abandoned old building. Rushing inside the building, they managed to lock the main doors. Michael fell to the ground and said, “I give up.” Tears started to roll down his face one by one. It was hard to see Michael in that state, especially because he was so young. Mirian felt useless as a mother because she felt as if she couldn’t do anything.

With a determined voice, Tami said, “All we have to do for our training session to be over is believe in ourselves.” She continued her inspiring speech by letting her family know that they were all special in every way, shape, and form.

Harvey interrupted Tami and put his right hand on his hip. He began to lecture everyone, telling them that their higher beings must have seen something in them that they didn’t. He also reminded his family about the powers they had on Earth. Talisha held Tami’s hand and said, “She’s right. All we need to do is work together and to use the powers that we knew we had.” Michael stood up from where he’d fallen to the ground and told everyone to hold hands and say a quick prayer. They did exactly that. Then they all opened their eyes and felt energised. They didn’t really know why, but they knew they were ready to take on anything.

Different objects started falling out of the sky, hitting the ground and creating what seemed to be half human and half robot. The way they moved was petrifying. Tami came up with a theory that everyone should touch her, as this would give everyone the opportunity to have an extra ability. Michael's ability was enhanced, and he could solidify and manipulate water that could be turned into ice. His power was only limited to his imagination. This instantly got everyone's attention when they saw the impact that it had over Michael. Mirian and the rest rushed over to Tami and grabbed hold of her arm. When they felt an electrifying energy charge through their bodies, it left them feeling fearless and energetic.

They all immediately focused on their opponents. Tami decided to make the first move when she started to throw electric energy balls at the human centipede. At this point she thought she had made the right decision by taking on the human centipede alone. But that's when she learnt that her fears were getting in the way of her controlling her power. With a fast reaction the human centipede reached out towards her and started to squeeze her very tightly. This caused Tami to become light headed.

This led Mirian on a path of destruction. Something inside her wanted to burst out as she saw her helpless daughter in the hands of the human centipede. She quickly raised her arms and somehow absorbed the light from the sky. And made the sky pitch black, which made it hard for everyone to see. A voice appeared asking Mirian to telepathically speak to Tami and tell her that everything was going to be okay. Mirian calmly told Tami and the rest of her kids to get prepared to use their powers. Even though Tami couldn't see her mother, she felt as if her mother was standing right beside her. Tami focused hard on her siblings, she focused on their faces and emotions. And with few seconds passing by, she began to feel light headed. Tami began to communicate with her siblings. Informing them about what Mirian told her to tell them. Everyone started to freak out when they hear Tami's voice in their heads. They eventually calmed down and took everything into account with what Tami was telling them to do. When she finished telling them what her mother told her, which was for them to get prepared to use their powers, Tami quickly communicated back to her mother telepathically, letting her know that everyone was prepared for the challenge.

As Mirian heard her daughter's voice inside her head again she slowly raised her arms and pointed to the sky. Suddenly everyone was able to see again, as it was visible for Talisha to see again. She quickly ran behind the human centipede and began to throw rocks at it. As the centipede turned its body towards Talisha, Tami quickly thought of a glass box and when she did it came into existence. The centipede was trapped inside the glass box. Tami quickly looked at Talisha and communicated with her telepathically. Talisha quickly touched the glass box and started to absorb the little oxygen that the centipede had left. Everyone watched as its lifeless body dropped inside the see-through glass box. Tami and Talisha began to smile because they started to fully understand what their powers were and how to control them.

Something in the distance caught everyone's attention, when they saw the half man half robot. It had a dog tag around its neck displaying the word 'humanoid'. Michael thought of something fast as he was running towards the humanoid. Mirian reacted fast by screaming out his name and ordering him to come back. Michael got the hang of speaking telepathically when he told his mother not to worry because he had a plan. Michael saw the sea in the distance whilst he was still running. Tanarla lent Michael a hand by teleporting the humanoid towards the sea while Michael was still running. When he got closer to the sea he began to gather a good amount of water and raised it above sea level. He started to form a spherical cocoon, and Tanarla took no chances as she teleported the humanoid in to cocoon. This caused the humanoid to malfunction which slowly decreased its oxygen supply.

Everyone felt confident with what they had accomplished so far, until they felt a strong vibration coming from the bottom of their feet. When they all turned around to see what was heading their way they saw two towering creatures that had chrome like skin with eyes all over their bodies. When Harvey managed to levitate off the floor he saw the same dog tag around their necks but displaying a different name. That said Tramerzonz, Harvey quickly shouted out the name that he saw on the tag.

As Harvey was making his way down from where he was levitating he felt a gush of air coming from behind his head. When he quickly turned to see what was behind him, the invisible being managed to punch his cervical nerve. Doing enough damage for temporary paralysis Mirian and the rest saw Harvey falling from the sky, unconscious. Tanarla quickly teleported from where she was standing to help her brother's lifeless body falling from the sky. As Tanarla teleported to the ground Morgan quickly ran towards them as she saw Tanarla crying. She touched her shoulders and told her that she can heal. Morgan quickly kneeled next to Harvey's body and touched the top his head, a numb subtle covering trickled down Harvey's pineal gland straight to his cervical nerve repairing the nerves. As everyone gathered around they were astonished by Morgan's healing abilities. When the Tramerzonz witnessed Morgan's healing ability, they quickly joined forces with the invisible object that broke Harvey's spine. The unidentified object made itself visible for the Hall family to see. And around the unfamiliar object's neck displayed the name autrolectrica. As everyone looked up and witnessed the object standing next to the Tramerzonz, Tami quickly reacted and gathered her family close beside her. She told them to join hands, and to close their eyes so they could only see darkness, Tami telepathically spoke to everyone including Harvey, telling them that she was going to be counting to five and after five, they would all need to open their eyes. When she had done exactly that they opened their eyes. Everyone saw this massive black hole appear right before their eyes; this was achieved by Tami using the energy from her family. This strategy was successful because everyone holding hands, which increased and locked the energy that was coming from their bodies. Tami somehow used a power that she didn't think she had and absorbed all their energy. This helped to create the worm hole.

This caused the Tramerzonz and the autrolectrica to get sucked in the black hole. Tami then told everyone to let go of their hands, and when they did the black hole closed. They all looked at each other gracefully knowing that they had passed the main test. The holographic world no longer existed, and they realised that they were back in the training room station.

After their successful training session, the Hall family went off with their higher beings so they could get dressed for their celebration. The females returned to the amazing room wearing a white and gold gown picked out by their higher beings. They saw a huge table loaded with many of their unique foods.

Most of them rushed to the table, leaving Mirian and their higher beings walking behind them. The preparation of the food was well presented.

They all waited until Mirian and the rest of their higher beings entered the room. The king and his daughter, Princess Valentani, hovered into the room. As they sat down around the table, the king looked at Fiona and Morgan with confusion because they were looking at the food with disgust. The king called over Milik and

Skylar, Fiona and Morgan's higher beings. They quickly hovered to the king, and the king asked them, "Haven't they tried our food before – because it seems as if the others are enjoying it more than they are."

They looked over to where Morgan and Fiona were sitting and then looked back at the king. They informed him that they ascended to Phenexus late due to complications that occurred. The king enchanted a spell beneath his breath. He pointed his finger to where the two sisters were sitting and flicked it twice. Their eyes glowed bright white for few seconds, and then Morgan and Fiona started to see their unique foods as their own on earth. In their eyes, they saw chicken, fish, pasta, rice, and desserts like apple crumble. The food might have looked unpleasant, but it sure tasted like the food on Earth. Everyone ate the unusual foods that tantalised their tongues. Talisha and Tanarla thought to themselves that it was something that they could get used to on a daily basis.

Teekalla and Brotacus waited for everyone to get well into the meal. And then began to congratulate every single one of them, on their success in passing the task. Everyone was talking amongst themselves when the king immediately got their attention by creating the name Phenexus from the different foods that were displayed out on the widely-built table. The king launched into tears of joy because he knew deep down how special every member of the Hall family was.

But Tami had other things on her mind because she was still wondering about the earth and how the planet affected millions of people based on the world turning upside down. She then built enough courage to get up from where she was sitting and started to walk towards the big gold-and-black double doors with unique symbols at each corner of the door, which looked like a key with unique patterns on the top of the door. Her family quickly looked to the right, where Tami was heading out, and began to talk amongst themselves. Then they asked where she was going.

When Tami heard the echoing voices from everyone in the room, she began to walk faster towards the doors so she wouldn't have to make eye contact with anyone in the room or answer any questions. Tami's higher being, Teekalla, had a disturbing feeling about Tami's unreadable acts, so she made the decision to absorb the energy from the sun. This led her to close the door so Tami would be unable to walk out. Tami stopped and turned her head to where everybody was celebrating. And said with a light and innocent voice, that she wanted to be on her own so she could have a quiet walk by herself.

Everyone then began to look at Teekalla to see what her reaction would be. Teekalla told Tami that she was allowed to go out.

Tami replied in an overwhelmed voice, "Thank you, so much." Teekalla then opened the big gold-and-black double doors with one of her unique powers. Tami rushed out of the room as if her life depended on it.

As Tami was still running, she felt her body getting tired, so she decided to slow down her pace. She then noticed some sort of symbol on a door that was quite similar to the room she was in. She made her way up to the symbol and touched it, which led the doors to open. She looked behind her to see if anyone saw her and then started to walk inside, which seemed to be an old library. It was filled with different books and weird-looking articles. Tami knew that she was in one of Phenexus's ancient libraries. Once she was fully inside the big and darkened room, the doors began to close in on her. Tami started to run towards the doors, trying to do everything in her power to stop them from closing. But it was too late, which led her to panic. She started to bang and kick the big doors. Her heart started to beat even faster, which caused her to breathe uncontrollably. But Tami remembered what she had to do in the training station to conquer her fear. She slowly started to control her breathing and to tell herself that she was fearless. When she realised that she was calming down, her hands started to glow. She thought that she might have been imagining things, but she wasn't.

Suddenly, Tami heard tiny flickers coming from what seemed to be the ceiling, and she noticed little blinking lights mysteriously floating on top of the spacious room. Tami began to squint her eyes so she could get a better look at the unidentified object, trying to work out what the little object was. Her vision became much clearer, which allowed her to see that the blinking objects were actually fireflies. Each individual firefly started to light up the room, making the same pattern that was on the door. Tami knew that it was possible for fireflies to create and display patterns, as they can regulate the airflow into their abdomens to create unique patterns. But she couldn't believe how accurate they were in demonstrating the pattern.

Once Tami got a hold of herself, she started to whistle, which created a light sound wave that attracted the fireflies, preventing them from coming down and flying straight towards her. Without any warning, Tami heard a light and gentle voice from a distance telling her, "Keep in mind that the fireflies that you see before you can sometimes be a deadly language of love." As she was looking around the room to see if she could see anyone, she couldn't comprehend what the voice was saying, but she knew it was telling her something. As the fireflies started to fly over Tami's, head, she noticed that they had the same symbol that was displayed on the door. She believed that a specific firefly was designed to open the mysterious room that was built inside the library. Then she thought about the voice that appeared from nowhere and what it had said. She saw one firefly that was in the shape of a heart. So Tami decided that she would somehow need to get the heart shaped firefly, as she needed to try and put the heart shaped firefly inside of the big doors that displayed the unique symbol. If she managed to get a hold of the firefly, then she would be able to see what was behind the big double doors.

She began to think of ways to attract the fireflies and bring them down. She began to whistle directly and gently at them. It was like a miracle; the fireflies flew down one by one. Tami spotted the unique firefly that stood out from the rest. As it was gracefully flying around her, she quickly grabbed the firefly and held it between her palms. She immediately ran towards the door with the same symbol that the firefly had on its back. She placed it directly onto the symbol that was displayed on the front of the big double doors. When suddenly it worked.

She heard the click of doors open deep inside the library, as she slowly creeped inside she saw something that caught her eyes. It had the word sitnalta written on it. It was a big thick book, and she began to take it down from the bookshelf. Once Tami managed to get hold of the book, she began to walk towards a sitting area. She slowly sat down and started to stare at the front of the book cover, feeling drawn to it. Tami slowly opened the book, and that's when she saw her reflection from a mirror displayed in the corner of the sitting area. It frightened her at first, as she thought it was someone else. Then she realised it was only her reflection. She noticed that the book that she was holding was spelling something completely different. The reflection of the book when faced directly towards the mirror spelt Atlantis, known on Earth as the lost city of Atlantis.

Tami was shocked when she discovered that the book was some sort of message. Tami was eager to know more, so she opened the book and started to separate the pages. It looked like an ancient book. The book gave reasons that the lost city of Atlantis sank. As she continued to read, everything about the earth and the planet Phenexus started to make sense to her. What she was reading mentioned Phenexus and how the planet XSoraya and Phenexus aligned. She began to skip pages and continue reading towards the ending of the book. Tami's right eyebrow rose due to the rare findings that she stumbled upon. Tami read the last few pages of the book.

When her hands started to tremble and sweat, she closed the book and made her way towards the door.

As Tami was heading out of the ancient library, different images and thoughts rushed through her head. And due to the course of desperation, Tami was willing to confront the king and the other higher beings. As she opened the doors, she entered a room of projected memories from her birth through the period when she was growing up. Tami became weakened when she saw those images.

Tami later discovered that she was born on planet Phenexus and not on Earth. This made her feel as if everything was a lie, right down to her family as well as her life. She felt a sense of anger and the desperation to know the truth. This led Tami to become frustrated and eager as she wanted to know the truth about her family and herself. Feeling betrayed, Tami rushed towards the doors, and as she was about to walk out of the room of secrets and truth, she found herself floating in the air uncontrollably. She started to flip from side to side, up and down. She began to try to balance herself. Failing to do that, Harvey was coming back from the toilets. She heard loud noises coming from the room opposite where he was standing. He slowly opened the wide doors when he saw his sister floating uncontrollably. Tami instantly felt a presence enter the room. Harvey called out her name, He was able to control the gravity in the room and to make things steady. He managed to get Tami down, as she barged past her brother with force, storming out of the secrets and truth room that revealed the truth about her past and her families.

Harvey followed her as she headed towards the room where her family was celebrating. Flashbacks began to flow through her mind, with different images replaying. Little tears looking like little crystals started to roll down her cheeks. When she got to the room where everyone was, she tried to slam open the big double doors to make a scene. But the doors were too heavy and thick to do so. Finally, she managed to open one of the big double doors. She stood there breathing heavily, and while she was looking around, Mirian rushed around the table to give her a hug. However, Tami totally blocked sight of her mother and focused on the higher being and the king.

When Teekalla noticed the emotions and expression on her face, she knew that Tami had been in the room of secrets and truth. The king gazed into Tami's eyes and said, "It's time to tell you the truth about what happened."

Brotacus got up from where he was sitting and said, "The king will tell you what happened three thousand years ago, with our planet and the planet XSoraya."

Tami's family felt disappointed and let down, and the thought of betrayal was rushing through all of their minds. They'd thought that everyone was being genuine and truthful towards her as well as her family.

Diamond said in a trembling voice, "I think you all should sit down for this."

As they all went to their seats and sat down, the king's expression told it all. His face had the look of despair. Tami knew deep down that the king and the other higher beings were keeping a dark secret from them. Out of nowhere, Tami exploded, starting to bang the table with frustration. She desperately wanted to know the truth about planet Phenexus and why there was so much information about her and her family up in the library.

The king began explaining to Mirian and the rest about the event that took place three thousand years ago. He started by explaining how his planet and planet XSoraya aligned every three thousand years. Everyone looked around the room to see if anyone knew what the king was talking about. But instantly the princess spoke over the king and said, "If you stop and listen to what Father has to say, then all of you will understand."

Everyone agreed to listen and concentrate on what the king had to say without interrupting. With a calm voice, the king spoke about what happened to the two planets when they aligned and how it affected Earth. He added that the planet XSoraya was the total opposite of theirs because its inhabitants dwelled on evil and negativity.

Princess Valentani knew that the king became nervous and uncomfortable when talking about the effect it had on Earth, so she decided to step in and explain, telling them about the horrific events that took place on the day of alignment. As Valentani took a deep breath to start her sentence, Tami interrupted her by saying, "I've had enough with all your delays, with the basic information about Earth and the alignment. I'll tell you the truth about what I found out about the events on alignment day." She started talking so fast that her mother had to interrupt her and told her to speak slowly so that everyone could understand. Tami listened to Mirian's advice and in a slower tone began to tell her family that she had discovered that when the two planets aligned, it somehow affected planet Earth, creating something called the blood moon, which humans considered doomsday. The special event that took place when the two planets aligned created something called a wipeout eclipse, which caused the whole Earth to lose light and energy. This normally happened because the sun blocked out any direct sunlight from reaching Earth, so this would give the beings from XSoraya the opportunity to descend to Earth and suck out the energy from any living thing.

The attention was stuck on Tami, based on the information that she leaked out about the two planets. She went on to explaining that she discovered a room with all their private information embedded inside it.

Teekalla covered Tami's mouth and told her to let the king have a say.

The king began to rub his head intensely as he started to speak about the effects it had on Earth and who they really were. He started his conversation off by saying that the last event for the alignment was very bad because it didn't just affect people's lives; it affected a whole city, a city called Atlantis, and caused the entire city to sink. The king told them that the people on Earth who ascended would need to be on top of where the water was. He said that they and others with the protection sign and charm bracelets were the ones who were chosen to ascend into Phenexus, and they could make the decision to stay and become protectors of the unknowing on Earth or descend back to planet Earth.

Teekalla added that the reason there was so much anxiety, depression, disasters, and earthquakes on Earth was because of the two planets aligning, their courses caused some sort of disturbance on Earth. And because this unfortunate event happened every three thousand years, that's what caused the lost city of Atlantis to sink.

Tami felt herself unable to move while she was listening to the hurtful truth. Fiona asked the king and princess of Phenexus about the planet XSoraya. The king told Fiona and the others that the Planet XSoraya is like Phenexus but the bad side of us, Teekalla added that it's a parallel world to their world. The goal of alignment day was to invade Phenexus with all that was happening the king finally came out with the truth. The

Hall family wasn't just chosen to be on planet Phenexus; they were actually born on planet Phenexus!

Everyone in the Hall family was speechless when they heard the truth coming out of the king's mouth. King Exous revealed the truth to them, explaining how they got on planet Earth and how their memories were erased so they would automatically forget so they could blend in with the other humans on Earth. After the king finished his explanation about who they really were, it was hard for everyone to look at the king as well as the other higher beings.

Talisha asked the princess about how they were born on planet Phenexus. She also asked a confusing question about the higher beings: "Are they us or not?" She believed that the higher beings were them – and that's why they resembled them.

The princess looked directly into Talisha's eyes with no emotion showing on her face and began to mumble words that didn't make sense. The king, who was also the guardian of Phenexus, took over. He said in a calm and soft voice, "The higher beings are actually your leading spirits. We call them Amorriious, or arcalactive beings." He added confidently that the Amorriious were the most powerful beings.

King Exous continued to talk about the higher beings and how Amorriious were created with every special person born on Phenexus. They were their spirits/guardians. The king then mentioned a name that was unfamiliar: King Tacorocks.

With all the truth coming out, Tanarla and Tami had the same question in mind, and they both asked their higher beings how they could only understand a bit of their language.

Teekalla responded to Tami defensively. “You do understand us; that’s how we communicate, with you as well the other Phenexians.”

But suddenly Tami remembered when the princess called out to her family when they first arrived, when everyone was sitting down outside that big beautiful garden and the princess said “abroo”, a word they did not understand at first. Tami said with a frustrated tone, “It was you, Teekalla, who had to translate for us what the princess said.”

The princess told her that it was the ancient Phenexian language that she spoke sometimes, mixing the old with the new language. Tami was satisfied with the answer that she got from the princess. Still, the room was intense and quiet because they were still trying to get their heads around what they were hearing.

With no warning, the sky turned red and a desperate voice from outside the building was yelling that the alignment was happening. The king stood up, grabbed his magic staff and headed straight outside, where he heard one of the Phenexians yelling. Brotacus and the rest of the higher beings followed him. Mirian and the rest made the decision to support them and followed as well. They all ended up outside, where all the beautiful buildings were.

Harvey overheard the king telling Brotacus and Teekalla that planet XSoraya and their planet had been aligning for some time now, as their planet had been slowly moving towards Phenexus. The king took a big gulp and ended his sentence by saying underneath his breath, "This time we can't lose anyone." Harvey was very concerned on how King Exous was acting. He was also wondering to himself how bad the effect could be on Earth when the alignment finished.

Harvey bravely walked up to the king and asked him the profound question that he was dying to know the answer to: would they have to descend back down to planet Earth to help the humans?

The king was happy to give him the answer. "You and your family will have to do everything in your power to use the skills that you learnt while staying on Phenexus and completing all the training station sessions." After King Exous said what he had to say, he gently placed his hands on Harvey's shoulders and told him to work together with his family because the power of energy comes from within. Harvey stared into the king's eyes with determination and told him that he would keep his words close to his heart.

After they finished their conversation, King Exous ordered the Phenexians to prepare for battle. As everyone began to put on the armour and battle suits, a disturbing noise appeared from nowhere, echoing above the sky. It was almost like a horrified scream, a big ship's horn blowing out of the sky. Everyone looked around with terror. Tami saw Teekalla from a distance and ran straight in her direction. As she got closer, her eyes started to change colour, her pupils split into two, giving the illusion that she had half-black and half-white pupils. When she saw the unique change happen right before her eyes, she paused and watched as all of the Phenexians' hair and skin changed dramatically. They completely changed their physical appearance, which made them look unrecognisable.

Tami heard her younger siblings screaming from a distance and knew that the rest of her family also saw the dramatic change in their higher beings and the other Phenexians. She ran to them and saw Michael covering his face as he also witnessed the changes. Teekalla and Brotacus approached the Hall family and told them that everything would be OK. Brotacus informed them those were their fourth senses and said that it happened when there was danger nearby so they were able to change their identities, making them as well as their vision a lot stronger. Tami and the rest knew that they weren't harmful; they knew that they just changed their physical appearance. The king couldn't be seen, but he could be heard, and he demanded that everyone stay indoors until they received a sign.

While they were waiting for the sign, it was very quiet as the alignment finished. King Exous rushed to the window and created something called a new entry sight, which was a special mirror that allowed anyone to see outside Phenexus. So in other words, they were able to see outside space when they used the new entry sight. They were able to see the white line that was adjacent to

XSoraya. The king said, "The light that you see before you is something like a portal with which the XSorayaians could ascend to our planet." The beings from XSoraya started to walk up to the light and abruptly vanished. The screaming that took place outside meant that they already ascended. Through telekinesis, the king ordered the Phenexians to put on their protective armour and to be prepared for battle.

Brotacus told Mirian and her family to join hands and descend on planet Earth so they could help out the humans, as the Xsoryasian planes were to invade Earth and take over. Brotacus demanded that they use their powers and work together because that's when they were at their strongest. They all joined hands and descended back to Earth.

While battling the XSoryasians, each of the Hall family used a skill learnt in the training station. They focused on their power, strength, senses, control of their power, and the most important thing: teamwork and leadership. Talisha became hesitant when she had to fight and use her powers. But with the encouragement from her mother, sisters, and brothers, she ended up with the right attitude. She hurried towards the XSoryasians and sucked the oxygen from their lungs. Her move made it much easier for the rest of her family to use their powers without being scared of the consequences. They all defeated the XSoryasians, which helped save the humans on Earth.

But there was still one big problem: the clouds were still on the ground, the sea on top of the sky. Tami, who had the power of dark matter, wasn't able to do anything, so she exploited her powers and used them to connect to Brotacus through telekinesis, asking him what they would have to do in order for the earth to go back to normal. He answered her question and told them that they would have to ascend back to Phenexus and help them out so everything could go back to how it was on Earth. Hearing the desperation in Brotacus's voice, she took the hands of her family members and ascended back into Phenexus.

When they managed to ascend, they saw that the battle between the Phenexians and the XSorayians had gotten very intense. It was so intense that they had to evacuate every woman and child from the scene.

Diamond created a portal so that the females would be safe with their kids. But Diamond was not alone; one of the XSorayians was analysing her every move. When one of them crept behind her just before the portal closed, one of the children shouted, "Cramzin!" This meant look out. When Diamond heard the little girl's desperate cry, she whirled around and saw her worst enemy, who was getting ready to execute her. She quickly created another portal which pulled the XSorayians into nothingness.

Diamond placed her hand into the portal and touched the little girl's face, saying thank you as she began to close the portal. Diamond began to look around, witnessing her home being destroyed and the people she loved the most being injured. She gazed into thin air and began to daydream about how happy everyone was before the disaster occurred. Diamond abruptly woke up from what seemed to be a trance.

She heard Teekalla's and Firestar's voices calling out her name from a distance, asking for help. She ran to them and saw them being captured by King Tacorock's son, Demor-i. He was so evil that he made the word *evil* sound holy. Diamond demanded that Demor-i let her friends go. But he was never the type to back down from a fight. He looked at her with a disturbing smile on his face and said, "Make me." Teekalla took something called a choker bean out of her pocket. This caused people to choke on their own saliva and pass out. She reacted fast and threw the choker bean directly at Demor-i. But in the blink of an eye, Demor-i's sharp instinct took over his body, and when he heard the sound wave of the choker bean leaving Teekalla's hand, he quickly responded by teleporting.

He made a portal in the direction that the choker bean was heading and created another portal behind, causing her to be distracted by it. Everything was moving so slow that it was like watching a movie in slow motion.

When Teekalla and Firestar saw the choker bean coming from behind her, they screamed from the top of their valcusses, the equivalent of human lungs. The floors began shaking uncontrollably, and Brotacus and Skyian knew instantly that Firestar and Teekalla were in some sort of danger. They both got the urge to stop what they were doing and head to where the vibrations became stronger. Firestar saw the two brave beings running towards them. Brotacus began to use his powers to release Teekalla and Firestar from Demor-i's trap. They hovered over to Brotacus, and when Skyian saw Diamond on the floor unconscious, he ran to her to see if he could feel her heartbeat. He felt a light beat beating in her chest. He knew instantly that he would need to find any Phenexian animal that might have been roaming around the area that they were in. Luckily, Flyars, which was the real Pegasus, flew in on the site and headed straight to where Skyian was holding Diamond. He leant over to where she was lying helplessly on the floor. Flyars's big innocent eyes began to water, and tears started to roll down its face and onto Diamonds chest. This created a pulse which healed and gave her a new power to heal herself and others. She got up feeling good as ever and began to use her powers against the XSorayians.

Brotacus reached his boiling point when he used his power on Demor-i. But there was something familiar about the two; they looked very much alike. Demor-i suddenly stopped the fight. When he told Brotacus that he knew the truth about him and his past, Brotacus paused and put his hands down by his side. He began to shout at him, calling him an evil liar. Demor-i called out his mother's name, Jarsaneea, explaining that his mother was a protector too, as Brotacus didn't really get to know his mother because the king told him at a young age that his mother was pulled into a wormhole and stuck between two dimensions. Demor-i told Brotacus that the king had lied to him. He asked Brotacus if he wanted to know the truth about his mother. His rage was no longer there when he asked Demor-i to tell him the truth.

Demor-I had an evil smile on his face when he started to explain that during the last alignment that happened, the Phenexians were getting ready for battle as usual. But on that day, she did something unforgiveable, which was betraying her own kind when the alignment finished. She made the XSorayians walk freely around her planet, and then she saw king Tacorocks and had relations with him. When he asked her to rule planet Phenexus with him, she agreed. King Exous found out what she done and what she was planning to do. So King Exous turned her into a tree that stood alone in the garden.

Demor-i's last words to Brotacus helped him understand why he had so much anger. It was because he was half Phenexian and half XSorayian. This made him understand why he felt a bit different from everyone else on his planet. No one else on Phenexus ever got angry, but he now knew the reason for his short temper.

When Demor-i saw Brotacus at his lowest point, he told him that he was his half-brother and part of their family. This led him to tears, and he placed his hands on his head. When he pulled himself together, his eyes went pitch black and he used one of his unique powers to crush Demor-i. As Demor-i was being crushed by his power, Brotacus walked closer to Demor-i and whispered in his ear, "My family is on Phenexus." He left the scene wiping his tears away and carried on battling what could've been his family.

Everything was starting to come into place as far as defending their planet and people when a loud and disturbing noise appeared from the back of the building. So Tami and Diamond peered up and created a wormhole big enough to suck up half of the beings from XSorayians. They then rushed to the back of the building, where they saw King Exous and King Tacorocks battling it out.

As Diamond and the rest started to run out of ideas on how to end the war, Tami turned her head to her right and saw Izion and Indigo dealing with their own battle. Tami spoke to her family and said, "We need to work together as a team, just as we did on Earth." Everyone agreed with Tami's encouraging words. They all separated and helped out with their new and improved powers, battling it out until there were only a few XSorayians left.

Everyone continued to work together until King Exous and King Tacorocks began fighting. The fight between them was hard to look at. The rage that Tami saw in King Exous's eyes was unexplainable. Brotacus came from a distance, shouting at all the higher beings, including the Hall family. They all joined hands so that they could gain power amplification to make their powers amplify and grow stronger. As they listened to Brotacus demanding everyone to join hands, an electrifying red shot out of Tami's hands and eyes, which led everyone to recharge, making them feel energised and fearless. The Hall family showed their worth to the king. When the individuals had specific colour electrifying through their body, differentiating themselves from each other, they began to point their fingers at King Tacorocks. Fire, water, electricity, ice, and other powers started to rush from their fingers, aiming at Tacorocks. This caused him to turn into electrifying ice; if anyone dared to touch it, then that person would be electrocuted.

Soon after that, the war was over. The king whistled for Jairan, which was Tami's cat on Earth, although called Jade there. He rushed down from beside the throne and started to decrease in size. The king held Jade and took off something that looked like a key around his neck and placed it where the light was joining the two planets. He whispered into Jairan's ear. The light disconnected, which slowed down the process of the alignment.

Everyone managed to survive the war; there were only those who were injured. With Morgan's healing powers and Diamond's new healing power, they managed to heal everyone on Phenexus who was injured. The king placed Jairan on the ground and looked around his kingdom, which was almost destroyed. He took a deep breath as tears began to roll down his face and smiled to himself because they'd proved to the king that he was wrong about them. They could be "earth-be-tectors". The king was delighted that the battle was over.

He used his magic staff to mend the buildings and to restructure his throne because it had been damaged. The rest of the higher beings and the other Phenexians helped out by creating a portal so that that they could bring the females and children out since the war was over.

The day after the battle, King Exous gathered all of them for a meeting to thank them for their bravery and participation. Due to the king's gratefulness, he gave them the options either to live on Phenexus or to go back to planet Earth. Mirian, being the leader as well as the mother, made the decision to stay on earth and have unlimited access to planet Phenexus. But she wanted to retain their title as earth-be-tectors because they always knew how different they felt from other people. Princess Valentani told them with a passionate voice, that it's in their blood to be earth-be-tectors. The king and everyone else accepted their choice. But they were also thrilled with their choice to have countless visits.

Everyone, including the higher beings, had a feast, danced, and played about. The warning alarms came on; it was the messengers between Phenexus and Earth sending out a signal to Mirian and her family so that they could help on Earth. Their higher beings equipped them with a new armoury. This sent a thrill down their spines, as it was their first mission together as a family. The king couldn't wait to tell the Hall family what would take place on their mission. He told them about the mysterious men dressed in black gowns with hoodies. There were reports coming in claiming that they were not human. They all started to prepare themselves to descend back to Earth, wearing the same electrifying red and other colours, which meant their auras were visible to the eye. Amazement was in their higher beings' eyes because they'd first started as seed and had now blossomed into beautiful flowers.

As years went by, the Hall family finally felt satisfied. They were all doing well. Tami graduated from university, and Mirian got a promotion from work, earning a lot more money. They moved into another home with much more room, loving and appreciating life just the way it was. They made a schedule that they kept in their house on the days that they all ascended into their second home, which was Phenexus. Life couldn't have been better. Morgan stopped getting bullied and made friends that she could trust, and Talisha created her own music band with her best friend, Alex. And Michael, Harvey, and Tanarla put their powers to good use anytime they saw a crime.

Mirian gathered her kids and asked them if they wanted to spend Christmas on Phenexus so they could see a new tradition. They all agreed to Mirian's proposal and ascended into Phenexus on 23 December. They saw their higher beings and gave them gifts from Earth. As Tami was giving her gift to Teekalla, Brotacus came from behind a tree and called out to Tami to follow him. She glanced back at Teekalla and gave her a signal telling her to go. And she went behind the tree where Brotacus's mother was placed. And that's when she saw a massive flower with the stigma of the flower sealed shut.

She asked Brotacus 'why is the flower so massive'. He touched Tami's shoulders and began to explain that

Teekalla was expecting to have his baby. When Brotacus finished explaining he began to touch and rub the floor. And told Tami that Teekalla and his baby were sealed inside the stigma. Tami quickly looked at Teekalla and rushed over to her so she could congratulate her, giving her the tightest hug. Tami ran off so she could tell everyone about how Teekalla was expecting Brotacus's baby. After everyone congratulated them both, the king and the princess called everyone in for a feast. They all made their way inside the huge building right next to where the king's throne sat to protect his planet. Everyone sat down and enjoyed the unique food that was presented to them.

The sky changed colour again, and they all heard the same sound they'd heard on the day of the alignment. The king stood up from his chair and used the new entry sight to look into space. He saw XSoraya completely gone and another planet appear. The king started to wonder if XSoraya might have replaced itself with a big new planet, but seeing his family enjoying the feast, he didn't want to alert them and get them worried, so he didn't mention what he saw or what he was thinking. The king sat back down at the table and ignored his thoughts as he started to talk to everyone and joke with them.

Teekalla and Tami felt that something was wrong, but they didn't want to spoil the feast. Therefore, they ignored their feelings and enjoyed the time they had with the king and the others.